A MISSION TO MENACE!

BEANO**books**

published under licence by

meadowside
CHILDREN'S BOOKS

THE TUTU TORMENT

Dennis was happy. It had been a very good day.

He had tipped a bucket of water all over Walter the Softy and his favourite teddy bear.

He had emptied a tin of tuna down the back of Minnie's neck.

He had put worms in the spaghetti that Mum was cooking for tea. And school had only finished an hour ago.

"D-E-N-N-I-S!" screamed Mum, when she saw her food wriggling. "Why do you have to be such a M-E-N-A-C-E?"

"Why can't you be a bit more like Walter?" Dad roared. (He was very hungry.)

"Who wants to be like softy Walter?" scowled Dennis.

"You do," Dad said. "And that's given me an idea! You are *going* to be more like him! Walter is never in trouble. From now on, whatever Walter does, you do. You and that Tripe Hound of yours."

"I'm not copying that flippin' softy!" Dennis said, bashing the table with his fist.

"You can start straight away," added Mum, pulling another worm out of her dinner.

"Walter goes to dance class tonight and you're going too. If you practise hard they might even let you be in the end-of-term show."

Dennis's mum longed to see him in the end-of-term show, just once.

"Dance class?" Dennis was horrified. "End-of-term show?

NO WAY!"

Gnasher growled. He didn't like the sound of this at all. Dad leaned over the dinner table. His tie dangled in his worm bolognese. He gripped Dennis by the scruff of his stripy jumper and pulled him up.

4

"You'll do it if we have to drag you there!" he blazed.

"No one drags me anywhere!" bellowed Dennis.

"Dennis," said Mum softly, "they have lots of free food there. Cakes and crisps and biscuits, and plenty of sausages."

Dennis thought for a moment. He could move faster than any of those wishy-washy dancers. He'd gobble down the food while they weren't looking and be gone before they even saw him.

"OK," said Dennis.

Mum winked at Dad, but Dennis didn't notice. He was too busy thinking about all those sausages.

Mum walked to the dance class with Dennis and Gnasher. Tinkling music was pouring out of the hall.

"You'll enjoy it once you're dancing," Mum said, and shoved Dennis and Gnasher inside.

"**Oi!**" yelled Dennis, but she locked the door behind him.

Inside, there were lots of kids in tutus, leotards and horrible pink tights. There were lots of pink shoes and matching pink bags. There was more pink than Dennis and Gnasher had ever seen in one place. But there was absolutely NO FOOD!

"**T-R-I-C-K-E-D!**" growled Dennis, grinding his teeth. He'd get them back for this!

Walter was in the front row, jumping up and down with glee.

He was very excited about being in the end-of-term show. He loved the pretty costumes and he could hardly wait to show off in front of everyone. When he saw Dennis he went pale. What was that nasty boy doing in his precious dance class?

Dennis and Gnasher stared back at him in horror. Walter was wearing a big, pink, floppy thing around his neck, like a necklace of petals. Lots of other kids were wearing them too!

"Are we all ready, flowers?" twittered Miss Tripp, the teacher.

"I am, Miss!" Walter cried.

"Oh yes Miss!" the rest of the class chanted eagerly.

"No!" bellowed Dennis. But no one took any notice. Gnasher growled and all his hair stood up on end. This was an emergency! The greatest menace of all time was not going to tiptoe around with Walter the Softy, pretending to be a flower!

Then Dennis had an idea.

Dennis's pockets were full of all sorts of things. There were bits of string and broken watches; dog biscuits and chewing gum; marbles and crayons; elastic bands and small screwdrivers. But they were mostly full of matchboxes. Matchboxes with *things* inside them.

If Mum and Dad had seen the look on Dennis's face just then, they would have panicked.

They would have dragged him out of the dance class as fast as they could. But Miss Tripp didn't know Dennis.  And she didn't know that look.

"We're going to practise the flower dance for the end-of-term show!" she trilled. "On the count of three!" She raised her hands in the air. A big grin spread all over Dennis's face. Gnasher was thinking whose socks to savage first.

"One!" Dennis put his hands in his pockets.

"Two!" Dennis's sticky hands closed around the matchboxes. **"Three!"**

The piano started thumping, the children started dancing, and Dennis opened the matchboxes. He dashed among the twirling flowers, emptying his matchboxes into their petals.

"**A-r-r-g-g-h-h!**" screamed Walter when he saw the fat hairy spiders.

"Eeeek!" squealed Bertie Blenkinsop, as the earwigs and centipedes scuttled down his neck. THUMP! went Miss Tripp, as she fainted to the ground.

It was pandemonium! Insects scattered across the floor. Everyone rushed for the door but it was locked. There was a pile up! Pink ballet shoes flew into the air. Pink ballet bags were crushed under stomping feet.

Walter got squashed and Jane lost her tutu. Gnasher went crazy with excitement – so many ankles to chooose from and so little time! Miss Tripp opened her eyes and found a big, black spider perched on her nose. She fainted for a second time. Dennis sniggered.

The dance class had never ended so quickly. Parents were called to collect their weeping children. Miss Tripp had to fan herself with Walter's petals. And as soon as the door was unlocked, Dennis and Gnasher made a speedy escape.

"You've ruined the dance for the end-of-term show tonight," yelled Mum, the next morning. "That dog of yours gnashed seventeen ankles!"

Gnasher looked proud and Dennis thought of all the kids limping home with bitten ankles, torn tutus and chewed shoes. He sniggered.

"You can wipe that grin off your face," said Dad. "I rang your teacher first thing this morning. You'll be doing exactly the same lessons as Walter today!"

Mr Dobson was waiting at the school gates. He clamped one hand on Dennis' shoulder.

"Good morning, Dennis," he said with a horrible smile. "You're not going to be in my class today. I expect you're as pleased about that as I am. Now don't be late for your first lesson. Hurry along!"

GRAH!

Mr Dobson pointed over to a classroom. The kids walking in looked pretty weedy and quite a few of them were limping.

"I'm not going in there!" Dennis roared, starting to squirm. Mr Dobson let him go and Dennis charged off. "Come on, Gnasher!" he yelled. But there was no answering bark by his side. Dennis turned around. Mr Dobson was holding Gnasher up in the air. Gnasher was writhing and growling, but he couldn't get free.

"That's a shame, Dennis," grinned Mr Dobson. "Never mind. I'm sure that Gnasher will still enjoy it all by himself!" He threw Gnasher into the classroom and shut the door.

"I can't let poor Gnasher take the heat!" groaned Dennis. He raced over to the door, yanked it open and burst in like a tornado.

"I knew he'd see sense," Mr Dobson said with a horrible chuckle.

Inside, Dennis looked around for Gnasher. The room was bristling with tubas and cellos, violins and recorders. It was music class.

"Hello Dennis, I've been expecting you," said Mr Plink, the music teacher. He was sitting at the piano and wearing a purple bow tie.

"Where's Gnasher?" Dennis demanded, scowling at the bow tie.

"Well now," giggled Mr Plink.

"We aren't really allowed to bring our pets to school, are we? So Gnasher is safely locked in the instrument room, and the key is here next to me. You can collect him at the end of the day. It's time you learned to obey some school rules. Now, let's make some beautiful music! Sit down there, Dennis. You can play the drum – one soft drum roll at the end, please."

There was nothing else for it. Dennis sat down and picked up the fluffy drumsticks. Walter was next to him, polishing his recorder. He frowned at Dennis. What was *he* doing here? It seemed as if Dennis was following him around.

"That horrid hound of yours ought to stay locked up – *forever*!" Walter whispered. "He's always scaring my darling Foo-Foo."

"Yeah well, Gnasher knows a softy dog when he sees one," hissed Dennis. "And no one can lock a Tripe Hound up for long!"

"Ready, everyone?" called Mr Plink. "We're going to practise the music for the end-of-term show. On the count of three!"

The class started to play the wettest, weediest music that Dennis had ever heard in his life.

PING went the triangles.

TINKLE went the xylophones.

TOOT went the recorders.

C-R-A-S-H! went Dennis on the drum.

He hit it so hard that the fluffy drumsticks flew right out of his hands. One plugged up the end of the trumpet. The other smacked Mr Plink right on his bald patch.

"**Excellent,**" said Dennis, and banged the drum with his hands. His fingers went straight through the skin. **RRRIPP!!**

"My drum!" screamed Mr Plink.

The trumpet player was swelling up like a balloon as he tried to blow the fluffy drumstick out. Then Dennis spotted a little mouse. He picked it up by the tail and dropped it PLOP down the front of the tuba player's blouse.

"**A-r-r-g-g-h-h!**" squealed the tuba player, who hated mice.

"Eeeek!" squeaked the mouse, who wasn't very pleased about it either. The tuba player let go of her tuba and started to jiggle about, trying to get rid of the mouse.

BANG! CRACK!

The tuba landed on the cello player, who lost his balance and fell into the string section.

TWANG! Strings popped and snapped. The guitarist sat on her guitar. **CRUNCH!** Dennis picked up the cymbals and crept up behind Mr Plink. **CRASH!** The sound made Mr Plink topple off his chair. He landed on top of the violinist and squashed her.

No one noticed Dennis's hand creep up to the piano. No one noticed him grab the keys and tiptoe over to the instrument room door.

The trumpet player gave a final puff. The drumstick end flew out of his trumpet and hit the flute player in the eye. The flute player stumbled back and fell over the violinist, who was just getting up off the floor. The violinist hit the flute player over the head with his violin and smashed it into tiny pieces.

Dennis unlocked the instrument room and Gnasher bounded out. They clambered over the pile of broken instruments and tangled bodies to the door. The room was ringing with groans and moans. Dennis turned and looked back. "No softy music at the end-of-term show," he chuckled to Gnasher.

Dennis and Gnasher hid and watched the musicians hobble out of the classroom to their next lesson. As soon as the coast was clear, they dashed over to the gates.

"And where do you think you're going?" asked an unpleasant voice. Suddenly Dennis was still walking but had stopped moving. Mr Dobson had the back of his jumper in a tight grip.

"School's not finished yet, my lad," continued Mr Dobson. "You've still got a sports lesson to get to, and you're late."

"I forgot my football kit," said Dennis, struggling to get free.

"Oho, that doesn't matter," chuckled Mr Dobson. "Football is much too rough for Walter. You're going to be playing netball."

Dennis turned and groaned.

Miss Toffy, the netball teacher, was jogging up and down on the spot. The netball class was behind her – twelve girls… and Walter.

"Oh no!" groaned Walter. He had a bad feeling about this. His knobbly knees began to knock together.

"Come along, Dennis!" called Miss Toffy. "Chop chop! No dawdling! I want you to be red team's Goal Attack."

If Miss Toffy had known Dennis better, she would never have said he could attack. He gave a menacing grin. "I'll show them how netball *should* be played," he told Gnasher.

As soon as Miss Toffy blew her whistle, Dennis snatched the ball off the surprised captain.

"Hey!" she yelled. "That's not…" But she went flying as Dennis rocketed past her towards the goal.

"*Bounce* the ball, Dennis!" yelled Miss Toffy, blowing her whistle desperately. But Dennis charged up the court, sending netball players flying left and right.

"Foul!" squealed Walter, as Dennis bounced the ball off his bottom and through the netball hoop.

THUNK!

GOAL!

Dennis whooped. Miss Toffy blew her whistle so hard that it flew out of her mouth and hit the team captain in the right eye.

24

"You're banned!" shrieked Miss Toffy as she looked at her battered netball class lying around the court.

"Fine with me!" grinned Dennis. "Come on, Gnasher! School's out for us!"

When Dennis got home he rushed into the kitchen, dumped his school bag and grabbed his skateboard.

"Hold on a minute," said Mum, picking the school bag out of the bin and brushing potato peelings off it. "I've got a surprise for you. Go and have a look in the sitting room."

"Cool! Is it a present?" Dennis asked. He wanted some stickers for his skateboard. But when he burst into the sitting room, he just saw Walter, who had a very large book resting on his lap.

Walter narrowed his eyes. He didn't want to be there at all. But his mumsy had told him to come over and he always did what he was told.

"Walter has come to show you his stamp collection," said Mum. "I think you should get a hobby and stamp collecting is nice and quiet."

"Some of these stamps are very rare," Walter simpered. "They come from all over the world. It's taken me years to collect them."

"Would you like a drink before you start, Walter dear?" asked Mum. Walter nodded and followed her into the kitchen.

Dennis looked down at the stamp book, which was lying on the table. Some of the stamps were really bright. He looked at his skateboard, then he grinned at Gnasher.

"Are you thinking what I'm thinking?" he asked.

Three minutes later...

"WHOOOPEEEE!!"

Dennis's mum was making a drink. Walter looked out of the window just as Dennis zoomed past the kitchen on...

"Is that a new skateboard?" asked Mum.

"MY STAMPS!" He's used them as stickers!" wailed Walter,

Dennis waved cheerfully at him as he sliced through Dad's begonias and left deep tracks across next door's newly mowed lawn.

"Oi!" yelled Dad.

"My lawn!" bellowed their next-door neighbour.

"See ya later!" shouted Dennis, as he disappeared round the corner at the end of the street. The last thing he saw was Dad jumping up and down on what was left of his begonias.

When Dennis came home for tea the kitchen was empty.

"Mum?" he yelled. But no one answered. The house was silent.

Dennis opened the sitting room door and went in. **WHAM!!!** Everything went black! Someone grabbed him and put a thick sack over his head!

"H-E-L-P! Gnasher! Kidnappers!" he shouted. But Gnasher just gave a muffled yelp. They'd got him too!

"Dennis, don't be silly," said his mum's voice as he struggled.

"Stop wriggling!" ordered Dad.

"Let me go!" Dennis bellowed.

"Not this time," said Dad, grimly.

Dennis and Gnasher were bundled into the back of the car. Dennis fought and kicked, but he couldn't get free. He was driven away, yelling at the top of his voice.

The car stopped and Dennis was picked up and carried. Then he was put on his feet. He heard laughing and applause. The sack was pulled off, and to his horror...

He was on the school stage at the end-of-term show!

Mr Dobson was standing next to him with a hand on his shoulder.

"Ladies and gentlemen!" boomed Mr Dobson. "I was supposed to be introducing Miss Tripp's dancing class and the school orchestra. But thanks to Dennis, they are not able to perform. So Dennis and Gnasher are going to put on a little show for you instead!"

"No WAY!" bellowed Dennis. There was a lot of cheering and more laughing. Dennis could see Walter in the audience with Foo-Foo. Walter was laughing and Foo-Foo was tittering.

"At last those two are getting what they deserve," Walter whispered in Bertie Blenkinsop's ear.

"About time too!" tittered Bertie.

Miss Tripp pirouetted onstage with two pink tutus. Before Dennis could stop her, she had tied the first one around his waist and the other around Gnasher's. The audience laughed and pointed.

"Enjoy the show!" said Mr Dobson, and ran offstage. Dennis turned to run too, but suddenly the whole netball class appeared in he wings. Every single one of them was carrying a netball!

Mr Plink was also in the wings. He grinned at Dennis, then pressed 'play' on the CD player. Tinkling fairy ballet music started to play.

"Dance, Dennis!" called Miss Toffy. Then the netballs started to fly at Dennis's feet! Dennis and Gnasher hopped around stage, howling as the terrible music played and they tried to avoid the balls. They was so busy dancing out of the way of the netballs, they didn't have time to take the fluffy tutus off!

The audience clapped and cheered as Dennis and Gnasher danced and leapt around the stage.

At last the music stopped and the curtain came down. Dennis and Gnasher pounded off stage, their tutus bouncing fluffily. Dennis's mum wiped tears of laughter out of her eyes.

"I'm sure Miss Tripp's class would have been wonderful," she chuckled. "But seeing the worst menace of all on stage in a tutu was the best end-of-term show ever!"

HUBBLE BUBBLE TROUBLE

Dennis was smiling, which worried Mum and Dad.

"What are you so pleased about?" asked Dad. "Am I going to have to pay for it? What have you done?"

"Nothing," replied Dennis. "Me and Gnasher are going to Curly's birthday party."

"I thought the party didn't start until this afternoon?" said Mum.

"It doesn't," Dennis grinned. "So we'll get to the food first!"

Dennis and Gnasher raced down the road. They spotted Pie Face coming out of his house.

"All right, Pie Face!" yelled Dennis.

"I'll race you to the jelly!"

Dennis and Pie Face sprinted down the street and crashed through a fence. Old Mrs Hubbard toppled sideways into the hedge. Little Tommy Baker fell off his toy car and five of the Colonel's favourite tin soldiers got trampled.

"I say!" trumpeted the Colonel. "Insubordination, sir!"

Dennis and Gnasher skidded through Curly's gate and up the path to his door. Pie Face was two steps behind. Curly opened the front door and Dennis sped through to the kitchen. Curly's mum was setting out the party food.

"Beat you!" yelled Dennis as he grabbed a handful of crisps.

"P-I-E-S!" cried Pie Face in delight.

"I-C-E C-R-E-A-M!" Dennis grinned.

"S-A-U-S-A-G-E-S!"

thought Gnasher, licking his lips.

"Help!" squeaked Curly's mum. There was a blur of grasping hands, sticky fingers and chomping teeth. Food flew through the air. Mouths opened wide. Gnasher bit ankles and gobbled whatever got dropped.

There was jelly on the light fittings. There was cake on the walls. There was ice cream in Curly's ears. Curly's mum escaped through the back door.

"Excellent snack," grinned Dennis, rubbing his belly. "Now it's time for the bumps!"

Pie Face and Dennis grabbed Curly and gave him double bumps. Gnasher nipped his bottom every time it got near the ground. When Curly stopped yelling, a big grin spread over his face.

"Presents!" he shouted. There was a big parcel in the middle of the sitting room, wrapped in silver paper and topped with a big red bow. Curly tore at the paper and found...

"Wicked!" gasped Curly.

"Brilliant!" Pie Face exclaimed.

"A chemistry set!" beamed Dennis.

Curly, Dennis and Pie Face pulled out the box. It was full of test tubes, beakers and a note which read.

SORRY, CURLY! KNOWING YOUR FRIEND DENNIS THE MENACE ONLY TOO WELL, WE THOUGHT IT SAFER FOR ALL CONCERNED IF THE CHEMICALS WERE REMOVED FROM THIS BOX.

SORRY!

Mum and Dad

Dennis smiled a 'you don't beat me that easily' smile.

"To the kitchen, pals!"

Dennis, Pie Face and Curly raced throgh to the kitchen and were soon emptying the kitchen cupboards and getting out all the biggest bowls. Dennis rubbed his chin thoughtfully.

"If spoilsport parents won't let us use real chemicals, we'll have to find something else!

"They're always telling us to do more homework – so let's practise some Chemistry! Some Worcester sauce, I think, Professor Curly. And the washing up liquid, Professor Pie Face."

Dennis poured the Worcester sauce into one beaker and squirted half a bottle of 'Super Strong Washing Up Liquid' over it. Then he added a glass of 'Lughole's Lemonade,' a dollop of 'Bogley's Best Strawberry Sauce' and five frozen prawns. The mixture bubbled and glugged, turned a strange rust colour and gave off a terrible stench of rancid rotting eggs.

It was like indoor fireworks!

There was a deafening explosion. Purple spray shot in every direction. The kitchen walls were now green with purple spots. Gnasher was black with purple spots. Dennis wiped purple goo out of his eyes.

"This is your best birthday present ever!" he grinned.

Dennis, Pie Face and Curly emptied the kitchen cupboards and got out all the biggest bowls. Dennis rubbed his chin thoughtfully.

"They're always telling us to do more homework – so let's practise some chemistry! I think the orange sherbert this time, Professor Curly. And the washing up liquid, Professor Pie Face."

"Pworrr!" groaned Pie Face, clipping a peg to his nose. "That's awful!"

"Terrible!" agreed Curly, tying a hanky around his face and grinning.

Just then Walter the Softy walked past the window with his friend Bertie Blenkinsop.

"Yeah, we should really take this outside," Dennis said with a menacing smile. They rushed out with the bowl.

"Fill water pistols!" commanded Dennis.

"Ready... aim... F-I-R-E!"

Three streams of rust-coloured goo shot at Walter and Bertie. They were covered from head to toe! The smell was overpowering! Unbelievable! Unbearable!

"Help! Help!" Walter wailed, rushing up to Sergeant Slipper.

"Get away from me!" roared Sergeant Slipper. "You stinky boy!"

"Help us, we're under attack!" squealed Bertie to the Colonel.

"Retreat! RETREAT!" the Colonel bellowed. "Where's my gas mask?"

Dennis, Curly and Pie Face rolled about on the garden, holding their stomachs and roaring with laughter.

"That was genius!" Curly chuckled happily.

"There's more where that came from!" grinned Dennis. They ran back into the kitchen. They grabbed some tomato ketchup and some green food dye.

"Red's a good start," said Dennis, pouring the ketchup into a fresh bowl. "But we need something black for a real menacing mixture!" He reached under the sink and found some engine oil. Then they added six marbles, three banana skins and a bottle of extra-hot chilli sauce.

"Time for an ambush!" Dennis ordered. There was only one place for that! They went to the Colonel's house and poured the menacing mixture onto the path.

"Colonel! You're under attack! Defence tactics!" Dennis yelled.

The door flew open and the Colonel charged out, but as soon as he stood on the path his feet slipped on the mixture! He skidded and stumbled on the marbles then landed THUMP on his backside.

"YOWE-E-E!!" he cried, shooting up into the air like a rocket. The extra-hot chilli was burning his bottom!

Dennis, Curly and Pie Face were laughing so hard they forgot to hide. "You young whippersnappers!" roared the Colonel, hurrying inside to bathe his burning bottom. "Court-martial! Five weeks in solitary! Half rations for everyone!"

"Come on," Dennis said, "we've still got some menacing to finish!" Back in the kitchen, Dennis added a tin of Cruddy's Cat Food to the green liquid.

Curly sprayed in a can of his dad's shaving foam and Pie Face tipped in Curly's mum's foot wash. They added ten spoonfuls of sugar and half a box of washing powder. The mixture started to shiver and shake.

"How about a nice surprise for my dad?" Pie Face suggested.

At Pie Face's house they poured the bright green liquid into his dad's car washing bucket and hid behind the garage. When his dad threw the contents of the bucket over the car...

KABOOM!!!

Green foam covered the car! It went up Pie Face's dad's nose and down his trousers!

"Pie Face!" he bellowed. "Where are you? Come back here!"

But the menaces were halfway down the street, almost crying with laughter. Pie Face's dad had so much green foam in his eyes that he couldn't see to follow them.

"That's the end of our chemistry homework," sighed Curly, when they stopped running. "We've used everything up now."

"Think again," said Dennis. He jerked a thumb at the building next to them. A little bronze plaque said:

PROFESSOR NUTJOB

MAD SCIENTIST

AND

OFFICIAL ECCENTRIC INVENTOR

"He must have loads of potions and mixtures," said Dennis.

They pushed open the front door and stepped inside. There was another door with a big notice on it that said:

> ### ABSOLUTELY NO ENTRY
> *THAT MEANS*
> ## YOU!

"Come on," said Dennis, opening the door and peering round inside. "It's totally empty. I think he must be out to lunch."

"Well, let's keep quiet," said Curly. He didn't want his pocket money stopped again.

"We'll just borrow a few things," whispered Dennis as they tiptoed in.

"Cool! Look at this!" Curly hissed. He had found a row of brightly coloured bottles on a shelf.

"**W-I-C-K-E-D,**" said Pie Face, forgetting to whisper. "What do they say?"

"Fast-Gro," read Dennis. "Your plants will grow in minutes with this amazing secret formula."

"Speedy Solution," Curly read, pulling down another bottle. "You will run like the wind and never be late for work again."

"Forty Winks," continued Dennis, reading the next bottle. "This will make you sleep like a baby."

Dennis filled his pockets with the bottles. Then they left the lab and headed for his house. Mum was in the garden, pulling up weeds.

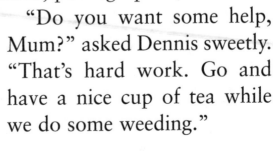

"Do you want some help, Mum?" asked Dennis sweetly. "That's hard work. Go and have a nice cup of tea while we do some weeding."

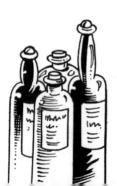

Mum stood up and glared at him.

"What are you up to?" she demanded.

"Errrr, nothing!" said Dennis innocently. But he slowly uncorked the bottle of Fast-Gro as she walked into the kitchen…

Mum had just taken a big gulp of tea when she glanced out of the window to see how they were doing.

"Arrgghh!" she spluttered. Her tea was showered all over the plants on the windowsill.

"Brilliant!" exclaimed Dennis.

The weeds were towering above Curly and Pie Face, waving in the breeze like small trees. The garden looked like a jungle!

"Dennis!" bellowed Mum. "What have you done? Get back here now and fix it!"

But Dennis and Gnasher just darted off behind a gigantic dandelion plant and out of the garden. Curly and Pie Face were right behind them.

"That was excellent," puffed Pie Face when they stopped running.

"What's left?" asked Curly.

"Speedy Solution," said Dennis, pulling out a bottle. "It says, 'shake powder on feet and you will run as fast as a cheetah'."

"That's what we need to get away from Sergeant Slipper," Curly sniggered.

"And my dad," added Pie Face.

"And this bottle is called... Forty Winks," Dennis grinned menacingly. "You know, poor Sergeant Slipper has been looking a bit tired lately."

He gave a little snigger.

They ran down to the police station and peeped in at the open window. Sergeant Slipper looked very busy filling out forms. (They looked just like Menace complaint forms to Dennis.)

"Right," he whispered to Gnasher. "You distract him."

Gnasher raced inside. He nipped Sergeant Slipper's legs and pulled at his trousers. While the policeman was trying to shake Gnasher off, Dennis leaned in through the window. He emptied a few drops of Forty Winks into Sergeant Slipper's cup of tea.

He grabbed the complaints, just in case any of them were about him (they were). Then he winked at Gnasher. Gnasher gave a final growl and darted out of the door.

"Blasted fleabag of a dog," grumbled Sergeant Slipper, sitting down again. "Someone ought to lock it up!" He took a big slurp of his tea and in a few seconds...

"Zzzzzzzzz! Snorrrrrrr!"

"It worked!" cheered Curly as Sergeant Slipper slipped sideways.

"A top bit of menacing," added Dennis, "and it's about to get better – here comes his boss!"

They watched the Chief Inspector stride into the police station. He looked very serious and important.

"Wait," said Dennis, holding up a finger. "My menacing nose can smell a row. One... two... three..."

"SLIPPER!" roared the Chief Inspector. The walls of the police station shook. "SLEEPING ON THE JOB, ARE WE?"

"I've been menaced!" Sergeant Slipper spluttered, groggily. "That dog was in here… it's all that Dennis boy's fault!"

Sergeant Slipper stormed out of the station with steam coming out of his ears.

"Stop right there, you pests!" he yelled furiously.

"I think this is the time for the Speedy Solution!" said Dennis, sprinkling it onto their feet and Gnasher's paws. There was a flash of black fur, a black and red jumper and four grins, then they were gone. The Chief Inspector came out and glared at his sergeant.

"There are no kids here! Menaced? A likely story! You can forget your holiday, Slipper – you need to find out what working *really* means!"

They stopped running when they reached Pie Face's house. There was someone at the front door talking to his dad. It was Professor Nutjob! Pie Face's dad looked furious. He still had green foam in his ears.

"Someone has borrowed my secret formulas!" blazed Professor Nutjob.

"*Pie Face!*" roared his dad. Pie Face panicked.

"Quick, do something!" he cried. Dennis reached a hand into his pocket and pulled out a small bottle.

"This is the last one!" he said. "Invisibility powder! Perfect!

He quickly sprinkled it over them all. Then they strolled up to the front door.

60

"We'll just walk straight past them," whispered Dennis. But Pie Face's dad started to stare. His eyes grew very wide. Professor Nutjob turned around and began to chuckle. Dennis looked at the others.

"Oh no!" he wailed. "That wasn't invisibility powder!"

"No," hooted Professor Nutjob. "My invisibility experiments have failed. The only thing I've been able to make is... fluorescent pink dye!"

The menaces stared at each other in horror. They were all covered in bright, glowing pink!

"Y-you mean you can see it in the dark?" stammered Curly.

Pie Face's dad rubbed his hands together. "At last, he said. "No more menacing for you lot until that dye washes off! That could take weeks! A brilliant invention, Professor!"

"Caught pink-handed!" smirked Professor Nutjob.

"Come on Gnasher, we've got to get home right now," wailed Dennis. "I never thought I'd say this, but I want a bath!"

SPORTS DAY

Dennis had tried his best to get out of it.

"I'm hearing voices," he said at breakfast. "I'm infectious. I've lost my toes. My brain fell out. Gnasher ate my sports kit."

"Only because you fed it to him," said Mum.

"And you're not getting out of sports day," Dad added.

Dennis groaned. Usually he loved sports day. He looked forward to the competitions. He looked forward to being the fastest and the strongest. Most of all he looked forward to getting as muddy as he possibly could.

But this sports day was going to be different. Mr Pump, the new sports teacher, had said that everyone who got muddy would have to have a hot, soapy shower afterwards. Dennis had argued and raged. He had tried every excuse he could think of. But Mr Pump would not change his mind.

There was only one thing for it. Dennis was going to have to avoid mud. And that didn't sound like any fun at all.

"I've never had to shower before," Dennis grumbled.

This was true. His old sports teacher had always been very glad not to have Dennis anywhere near the shower room.

"Well, your new teacher must be very keen," said Mum. "Anyway, it's about time you had a wash. I've given up trying to get you into a bath."

Dennis scowled.

"Now," Mum continued, "I want you to try your best today, Dennis. We'll be watching you, cheering you on..."

"...and making sure you don't get up to any menacing," Dad finished.

Later that morning Dennis stood outside the boys' changing room, glowering. There must be some menacing way he could put a stop to sports day. He reached into his pocket and his hand closed around a small tin.

"Perfect," grinned Dennis. It was his spare tin of itching powder. He crept into the teachers' changing room and saw Mr Pump's shorts hanging on a peg. Dennis emptied his tin into the shorts and smiled.

Once his teacher put those on, he would not be able to stand still, and without him sports day would be cancelled. Dennis went back to his changing room and waited for the good news.

But when Mr Pump strode into the boys' changing room, he was wearing a tracksuit! Dennis frowned. His first menace was ruined. What next?

Mr Pump watched as everyone shuffled out to the sports field. He was tall and tanned, with a huge chest and enormous muscles. His legs were like tree trunks and his head was large and square. Even the other teachers kept away from him.

"He's much too keen for this school," snarled Mr Dobson.

"He told me he loves teaching," complained Mr Plink. "The man must be mad."

"I heard him say he likes the children," added Miss Toffy. "Completely unnatural."

"He'll never last," barked the headmistress.

All the parents were arriving and waving to their children. Dennis saw Mum and Dad and scowled at them.

"R-I-G-H-T,"
shouted Mr
Pump through
his microphone. Everyone
winced and covered their
ears. "The first event will be
the egg-and-spoon race!"

The ten kids who were taking part stood on the starting line with their spoons. Some of them looked eager. Some of them looked miserable. Dennis looked furious.

Mr Pump walked along the row, putting an egg into every spoon from his basket. Dennis was the last to get an egg. Mr Pump put the egg basket down next to him.

"Mistake number one," grinned Dennis. If he couldn't get sports day cancelled, perhaps he could get himself banned from it! He reached down to the egg basket. Mr Pump held the starting pistol up in the air.

"On your marks!"

Dennis grabbed handfuls of eggs.

"Get set!"

Dennis got his throwing arm in position.

"GO!"

Nine kids surged forward, balancing their eggs. One menace stayed still and fired.

POW!

Plug fell down and cut his knee on some eggshell.

SPLAT!

Smiffy tripped and smashed his egg.

BONK!

Cuthbert was knocked dizzy by a hard-boiled egg.

Dennis kept firing until the only egg left was the one in his spoon. He stepped over the yolk-splattered children and crossed the finish line. The crowd hissed.

"That was not how you run an egg-and-spoon race!" shouted Mr Pump. "These children will have to go home – they aren't fit to join in any more events!"

"Am I going to be banned?" asked Dennis hopefully.

"Oh no," smiled Mr Pump. "I'm not that cruel!"

Dennis sighed. Menace number two hadn't worked. What now?

"It's the high jump next!" Mr Pump announced. "Line up, everyone taking part! Dennis, hold the mat steady please."

There was a big mud puddle right next to the thick blue mat. As soon as the first competitor vaulted over the bar, Dennis would get splattered! He pulled the mat across to cover the puddle, just as Bertie Blenkinsop started his vault.

B-U-M-P-!

Bertie landed on the hard ground.
"Owwww! My botty!" Bertie squealed. **"Silly boy,"** snapped Mr Pump. "How did you miss the mat? Next!"

Spotty was next, but just then Dennis saw another muddy puddle. He tugged the mat again. **C-R-U-N-C-H-!** Spotty landed on his nose.

There were dozens of muddy puddles! Dennis pulled and tugged at the mat to try to cover them all. **C-RA-C-K!** Curly landed on Spotty.

E-E-K! Pie Face fell face down in the mud.

"Very poor show!" frowned Mr Pump as Pie Face limped off to the shower room. "Your turn, Dennis."

Dennis glowered at the sports teacher and started to run up to the bar. But as he ran he saw another huge puddle – right in front of him! He shoved the pole into the ground and vaulted high over the bar, landing WHUMP in the middle of the mat.

"Very good!" said Mr Pump. "The winner of the high jump is… Dennis!"

"Well done!" called a proud Mum and Dad.

"Boo!" shouted everyone else.

"Next it's the cross-country race," boomed Mr Pump.

"Oh no," groaned Dennis. There

was nothing he liked better than splashing through deep muddy fields. But he wouldn't go into those showers!

"This could take a while," continued Mr Pump, "so there are some refreshments for the parents in the gym."

This was what the parents had been waiting for. There was a stampede for the gym. No one saw the race start. And no one saw Dennis sneak off in completely the wrong direction.

Dennis spotted Mr Pump's mountain bike in the staff car park. He rubbed his hands together. "I think I'm getting one of my brilliant ideas."

The kids running over the muddy fields just saw a blur as Dennis whizzed past them on the mountain bike. He stopped at the first crossroads and chuckled. There was a big sign that said 'cross-country runners this way' and an arrow pointing left.

"How about a little detour?" Dennis grinned. Just because he couldn't get muddy, it was cruel to stop the others getting good and dirty! He turned the arrow so it was pointing right, towards the Beanotown Bog. Then he took the left turn and sped off on the bike.

There was another sign at the next crossroads. Dennis pointed the arrow towards the woods. "It's so easy to get lost round here!" he sniggered. If there were no kids left to compete, they would have to end sports day! And he was still mud free!

81

When he got back to school, Dennis put the bike back in the staff car park and then jogged over the finish line. All the parents were just coming back from the gym, clutching lemonade and cake.

"Oh I say!" shouted Mr Pump. "Dennis has won the race! And amazingly, he has no mud on him!"

"I can hardly believe it," gasped Mum.

"Neither can I," said Dad grimly. "Not at all."

Mr Pump looked for the rest of the runners. But no one else came over the finish line. (This was not surprising. Seven of them were wading through a bog and two more were lost in the wood.)

"They can't have gone the wrong way," said Mr Pump. "Very strange – I put some very big signs up.

Anyway, let's get on with the next event – the long jump!"

There were only two children doing the long jump – Dennis and Walter. Dennis groaned when he saw the sand pit. It was full of rainwater and the sand was a muddy mess.

"Now, you know the rules,"

shouted Mr Pump. "Take a running jump into the sand. Whoever jumps farthest is the winner. **Good luck!**

You're first, Dennis!"

"There's only one thing for it," Dennis grinned. He hurtled down the runway and whizzed into the air over the sand pit. He jumped so far that he landed on the grass on the other side!

"Astonishing!" said Mr Pump. "I've never seen anything like it! Next please!"

Walter was next. He did some warm-up exercises as Dennis smirked and emptied his pockets into the sand.

"Good luck, Walter!" he called. Walter ignored him. He tottered down the runway, tripped over a daisy, looked down and...

"A-r-r-g-g-h-h!"
screamed Walter, trying to keep running in mid air. "Creepy crawlies!"

The muddy sandpit was alive with spiders, worms and beetles. Walter scrabbled out of the sand and kept running.

"COME BACK!" shouted Mr Pump. "Come back or you'll be disqualified!"

But Walter ran into the audience and hid under his mumsy's chair.

"Tch, tch," Mr Pump shook his head. "Odd boy."

There were only two kids left in the whole sports day competition – Dennis and Roger the Dodger.

"Only one to go and it's all over – without needing a shower!" chuckled Dennis.

"Next event!" announced Mr Pump. "It's the shot put! Dennis, would you go first, please?"

"Oh dear," said Mum.

"At least it's not the javelin," muttered Dad.

Dennis grabbed the shot and started to spin, Round and round he went, faster and faster, until he launched the shot. It flew through the air...

...towards the parents...

"Good throw!" cried Mr Pump.

"Bad throw!" shouted Mr Pump

...and squashed Walter's mumsy's picnic lunch.

"GOAL!"

cheered Dennis, punching the air.

He held the second shot out to Roger, but dropped it. The shot landed on Roger's left foot.

E-E-E-K-!

shrieked Roger, hopping around the field and clutching his foot, which was swelling up like a balloon.

Oops, butterfingers,"

said Dennis.

Mr Pump frowned. He was starting to think that this hadn't been a success. Slowly he picked up his microphone.

"There are supposed to be five more events," he said. "But there are no more children to compete. Since Dennis is the only one left – I suppose he is the winner!"

Just then Dad came marching up to Mr Pump. He said a few words. Mr Pump nodded vigorously. They both glanced at Dennis. Then they shook hands.

"Step up, Dennis!" bellowed Mr Pump into his microphone. "You are the winner of this year's school sports day."

Mr Pump took out a big gold medal on a long red ribbon. He put it around Dennis's neck.

Mum clapped. No one else did.

"Thanks," grinned Dennis. He turned to leave, but something stopped him. Mr Pump had tightened the ribbon around his neck. Dennis couldn't move.

"Not so fast!" he thundered. "Ladies and gentlemen, we have a special treat for Dennis. He's such a sporty lad, I'm sure he'd love to do some more exercise. So we're going to let him exercise his hands and knees. Dennis, you can spend the rest of the day cleaning out the shower room – with a toothbrush! And when it's clean, then you can test it out by having a nice, hot, soapy shower!"

There was a huge cheer from the crowd. The parents clapped. The children limping back from the cross-country race whistled and waved. Mr Pump got a standing ovation as he marched Dennis off to the shower room.

The other teachers looked at each other.

"Perhaps we were a bit hasty about Mr Pump," said Mr Dobson.

"He seems like a very nice man," Miss Toffy nodded.

"A splendid addition to the school," agreed Mr Plink.

The headmistress watched Mr Pump hand Dennis a toothbrush.

Then she did something very unusual. She smiled.

"I think he's going to fit right in," she said.

Written by RACHEL ELLIOT

Illustrated by BARRIE APPLEBY

published under licence by

185 Fleet Street, London, EC4A 2HS